The Music Makers

Contents

Written by Lara Jennings

Illustrated by Sue Downing

Collins

1 Anyone can make music ...

... it's just putting sounds together in whichever way you choose.

So, if you can make sounds, you can make music.

Some music makers are confident and love showing off. Others are shy and always get stage fright. Some are disabled, blind or deaf. And many have never had a music lesson in their whole life.

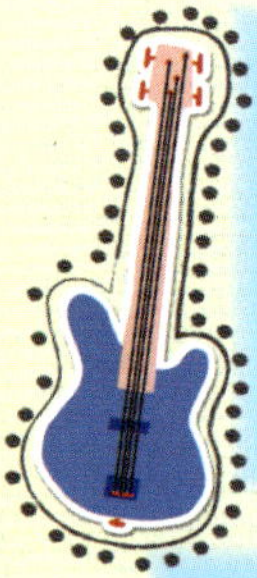

And you probably know what music you like, too.

Music makers just know when they hear something they like.

Maybe you don't know if it's **K-pop**, hip-hop or folk-rock. Maybe you can't explain why you like it … you just feel something inside when you hear it.

Well, this book is especially for you, music fan!

Did you know?

R&B star Beyoncé can speak fluent French.

Legendary soul singer Aretha Franklin taught herself to play piano.

The world's fastest rapper can rap more than 400 words in one minute!

Rock band The AutistiX are named after their autistic members.

Pop singer Olivia Rodrigo is half-deaf in her left ear.

Singer-songwriter Ed Sheeran wrote the hit *Thinking Out Loud* in 20 minutes!

SEAT

2 Crank it up!

SEAT 2

Pop

Short for "popular", pop often appeals to younger people and has a beat that gets you dancing.

Hip-hop

An energetic style that combines singing or rapping with rhythmic beats.

R&B

Short for "rhythm and blues", R&B often features catchy tunes and soulful singing.

Rock

Usually played by a band, with a singer, drummer and one or more guitarists.

Music map

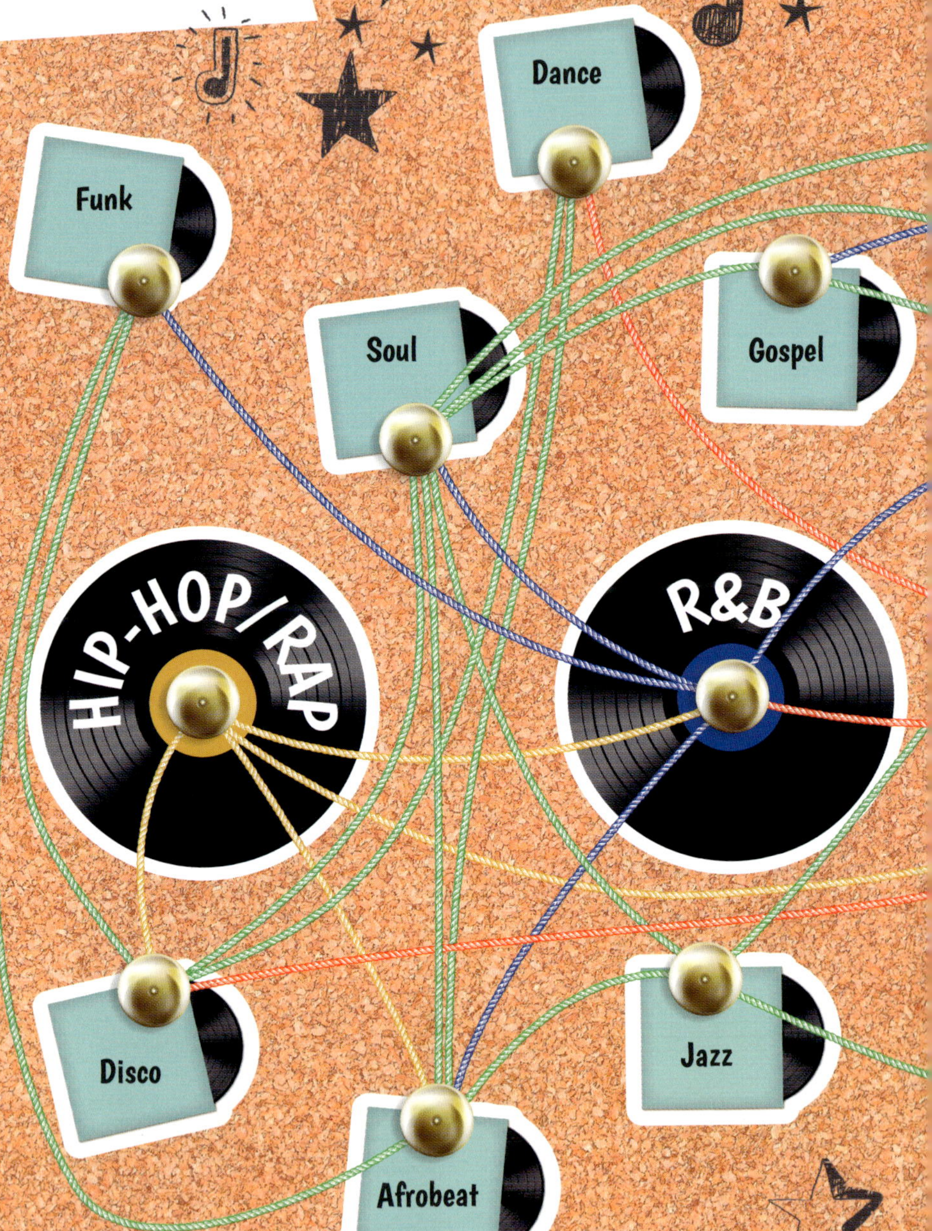

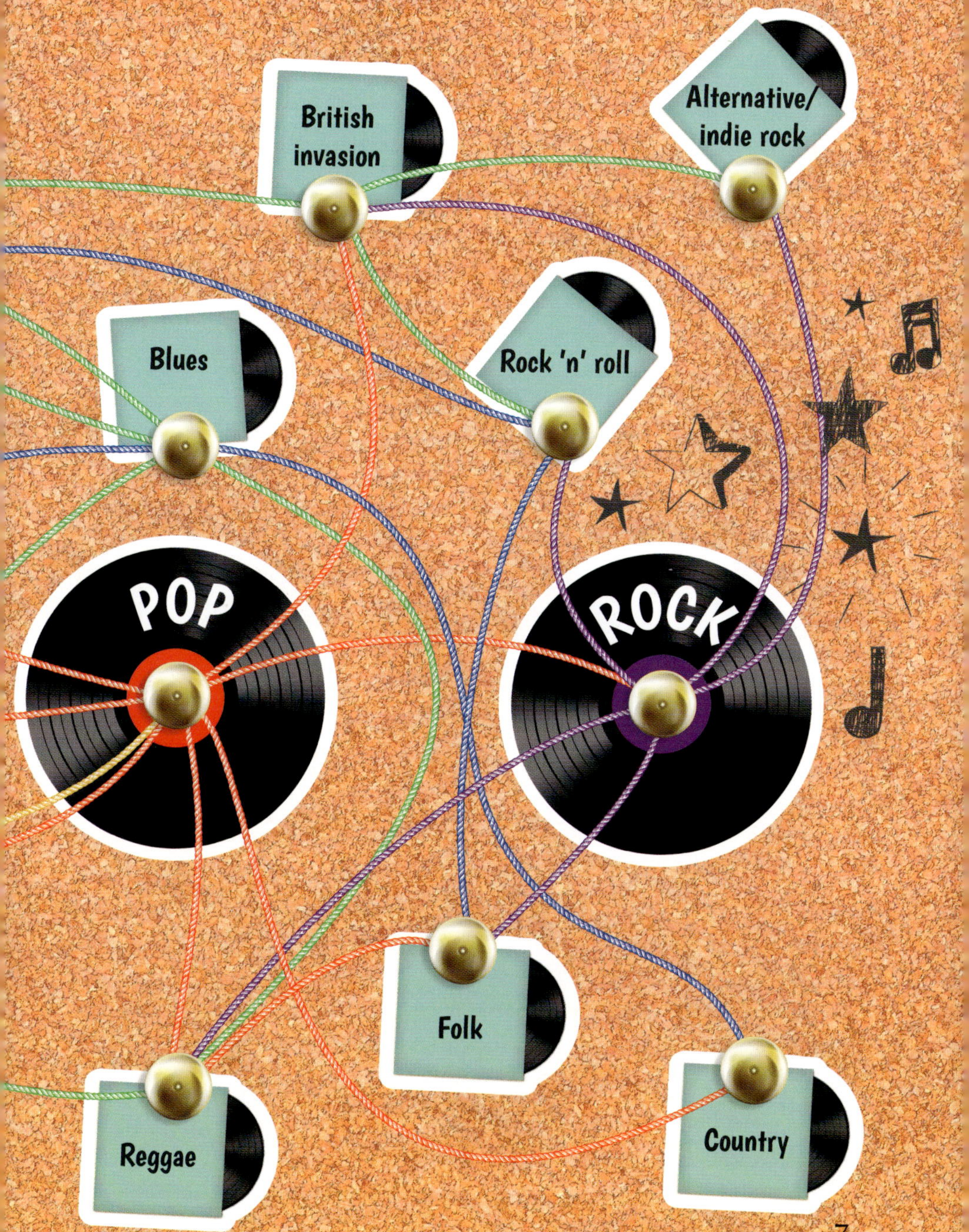
British invasion
Alternative/ indie rock
Blues
Rock 'n' roll
POP
ROCK
Folk
Reggae
Country

3 Meet the music makers

SEAT 3

Taylor Swift

This American pop sensation wows fans all over the world with her pure voice and **heartfelt** songs.

Ariana Grande

First performing in public at just eight years old, this American pop singer has made tons of records and won heaps of awards.

Harry Styles

The British pop singer started out by covering songs on his home karaoke machine ... and today, he's a global megastar.

Florence + The Machine

Meet Florence, the British singer with a super-powerful voice, and The Machine, her indie-rock band.

BTS

This Korean-pop boy band inspires fans around the world to dance to the beat of their own drum. All the group's members help to write their songs.

David Bowie

The iconic rock singer-songwriter from London. With his constantly changing image, Bowie showed the world that people can look and dress however they choose.

Beyoncé

Mega-famous R&B singer-songwriter. Aged seven, Beyoncé won a talent show for her singing. And today, *Rolling Stone* magazine calls her the greatest singer ever!

Jurassic 5

This legendary American rap crew are famed for their retro sound. Their beats make you want to jump up and dance!

The Beatles

They're your grandparents' favourite band ... but they're way cooler than you'd think. This legendary British rock group have influenced artists across most music styles.

Stevie Wonder

This American soul legend sings, writes songs and plays multiple instruments. He's also blind and has ADHD.

Nina Simone

Known as the Queen of Soul, Nina Simone poured her heart into every note she sang and played on her piano.

Who's your favourite music star?

4 I want to be a ...

Music journalist

You're the storyteller of the music industry.

You'll interview stars, review concerts and write articles that bring music to life. In this way, you'll play a key role in keeping fans entertained.

Manager

You're the superhero behind the scenes, taking care of the business side and making sure everything runs smoothly.

Without you, the performer might not even make it onto the stage!

Songwriter

In this job, you'll write awesome songs and collaborate with singers (hopefully your favourite ones!).

Many songwriters work from their own home. Here, they spend loads of time listening to other people's tunes, trying to figure out what makes them sound so good.

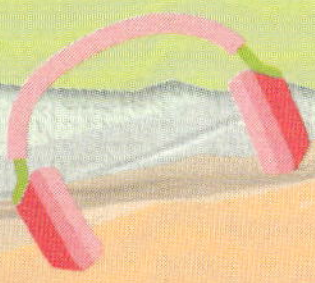

Booking agent

You'll arrange for musicians to perform at amazing venues. You'll also handle things behind the scenes, like travel arrangements.

Above all, you'll help artists give performances that fans will never forget!

A day in the life

Dewan-Dean Soomary, Music Producer

Where do you work?

My home in Texas, America.

What do you do each day?

Sometimes I'm up and down, plugging stuff in and unplugging. Sometimes I'm just sitting at the desk with a keyboard, like any desk job.

How does your morning start?

I walk my dogs and consider what's what. Is there something I need to do, like a **remix**? Or is there something I want to do, like working on a new album? If so, how does that start – from a guitar, drum machine, lyrics ... or something else?

Do you have much contact with music stars?
Yes! Face-to-face, video calls, sometimes just on email. It's kind of fun getting to know someone through music.

What gets you through the day?
My belief that there's no right or wrong with making music. You can do whatever you want. Some things can be taught … but self-expression is at the heart of it all.

What's your advice for someone dreaming of becoming a music producer?
Love making music. Fame is **fleeting** … just be in love with the joy music brings!

SEAT

5 Sing it!

SEAT 5

There are four main voice types:

- really high (soprano)
- high (alto)
- low (tenor)
- really low (bass)

What's my range?

It's the group of notes you can comfortably sing, from lowest to highest.

Chest voice or head voice?

Your chest voice is produced in your throat and chest, making a deeper sound. Your head voice is produced in your throat and the upper part of your head, creating a higher sound.

What's a harmony?

It's when music makers blend different notes together, often using their voices.

Why do singers use autotune?

They use this digital tool to correct out-of-tune notes. It can also give their voice a robotic, futuristic feel.

What's a rap battle?

It's where rappers go head-to-head, exchanging clever rhymes and showing off their skills in front of a crowd.

6 Play it!

Guitar

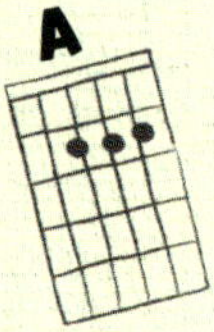

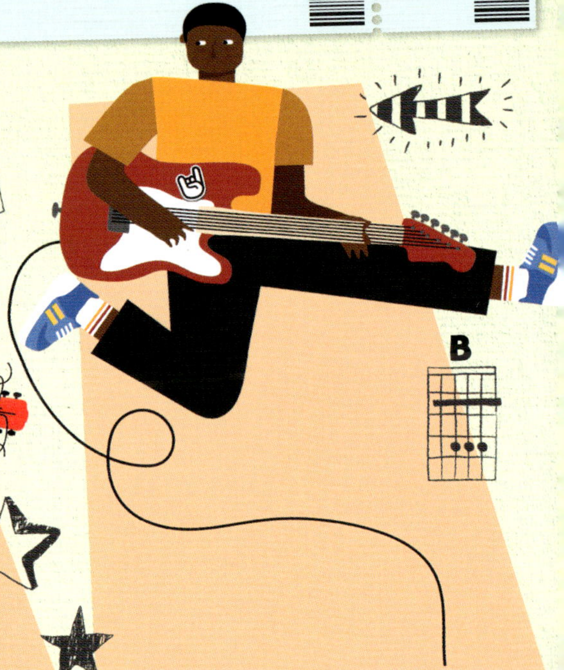

Acoustic: Six strings. 20 **frets**. One cool instrument.

Electric: Plug into an **amp**, strum the six strings and rock out!

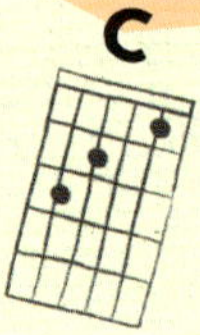

No instrument? No problem!

Many artists use music-making apps. These allow you to create tunes on your computer or mobile. They include virtual instruments and are often totally free!

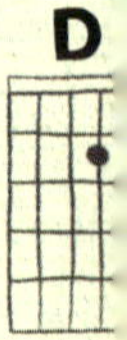

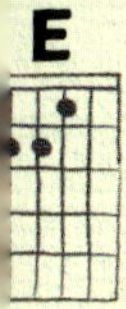

Plucking or strumming?

Plucking is playing individual strings. Strumming is sweeping across multiple strings. Guitarists often do both.

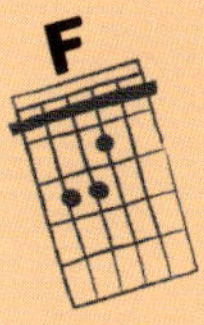

Bass: Blast out deep, booming sounds on the four strings.

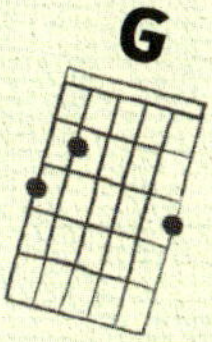

"I taught myself guitar from videos, books and advice from friends. If you want to learn an instrument, find someone who plays it and ask them loads of questions!"

Oh My Empress, singer and guitarist

Keyboard

The soft keys invite your fingers to glide from one note to the next. And the choice of sounds allows you to create any mood at the touch of a button.

Borrow it!

Could you borrow an instrument from someone you know – a family member, perhaps? Their old instrument might turn you into the next new music star!

Trumpet

Blow into the mouthpiece and the air vibrates through the metal tube to create a vibrant buzz of sound.

Drums

These create the rhythm of a song – whether it's the traditional thump of a standard kit or the futuristic beats of electric drums.

Can you make up music on the spot?
Absolutely! You can start from scratch or add your own bit to a song you know. You choose!

7 Peep inside a recording studio

Live room
where music makers perform

Control room
where the producer uses high-tech equipment to create the music

1 Producer oversees the recording, working with artists to perfect their track

2 Outboard gear used to perfect sound before it's recorded

3 Studio monitors for hearing the music

4 Speakers for hearing electronic instruments

5 Music-star sofa

6 Mixing desk where engineers blend different sounds to create a song

7 Engineer operates the recording equipment, mixes tracks, and captures the best sound from musicians

Become a bedroom artist

Lots of artists record their music in their own home, like singer-songwriter Billie Eilish.

Here's how you can do it:

1 Grab yourself a computer or mobile.

2 Download a music-recording app (these are often free).

3 To record your singing, use a microphone (one that's built into either a computer or mobile headphones).

4 If you're playing an electric instrument, record this by connecting it to your device.

5 Keep singing (and playing) until you've recorded your tune!

Peep inside a concert venue

1 **Monitor** allows the performers to hear themselves

2 **Speaker**

3 **Pedals** these alter the sound of electric guitars, adding effects like echoes

4 **Guitarist**

5 **Amplifier**

6 **Bassist**

7 **Microphone**

8 **Singer**

9 **Drummer**

10 **Keyboardist**

11 **Flat screen** showing pre-recorded images

12 **Sound desk** where the audio engineer tweaks the sounds of instruments and voices

"We walked on stage and were hit by applause, cheering and screaming from a mass of people. An unbelievable rush – I was absolutely hooked!"

David Ford, singer-songwriter

SEAT

8 How to name your band

SEAT 8

- **Reflect your musical sound**
  Example: The Funkees

- **Stand out from the crowd**
  Example: alt-J

- **Start with "The"**
  Example: The Pet Shop Boys

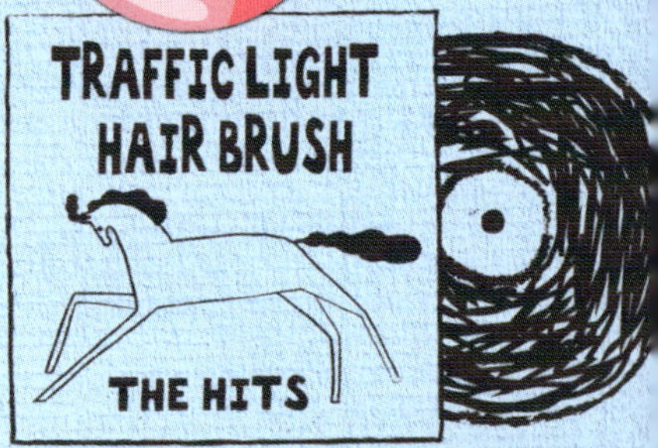

- **Combine random words**
  Example: Porridge Radio

- **Include your own name**
  Example: Joan as Police Woman

"I was in a group with my school friends. The other kids would say 'I hear you're in a so-called band?' – that's why we named ourselves So Called."

Richard Holley, singer-songwriter

What would you call your band?

9 How to write a song

Mix together different ingredients, like these:

- **main tune** (melody)
- **words** (lyrics)

- **chords** (musical notes played together)
- **rhythm** (beat and pattern of the notes)
- **hooks** (catchy parts of a song)

Usually, songwriters start with one of these ingredients, adding more bit by bit.

There's no right or wrong – just explore what sounds good to you!

What's a scale?

A group of notes that goes up or down in a certain order.

Different scales can make you feel different emotions.

In a major scale, the notes often sound happier.

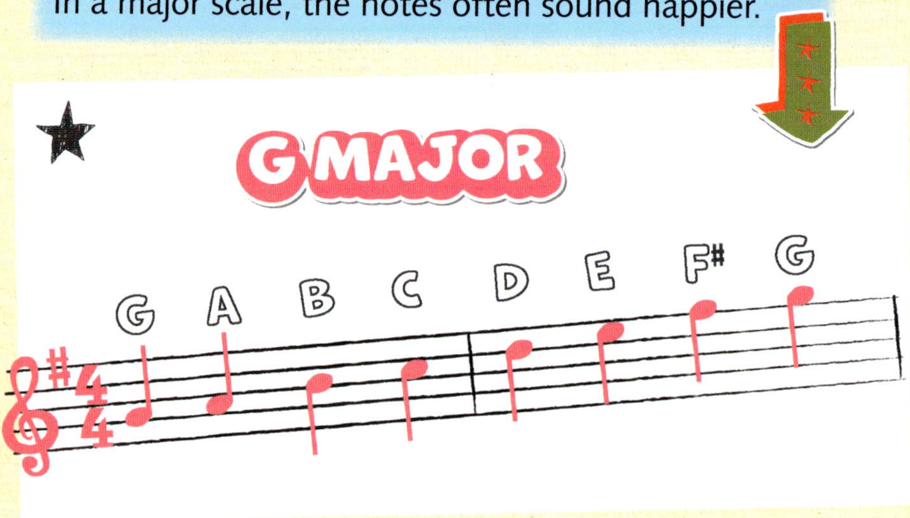

In a minor scale, the notes often sound sadder.

E MINOR

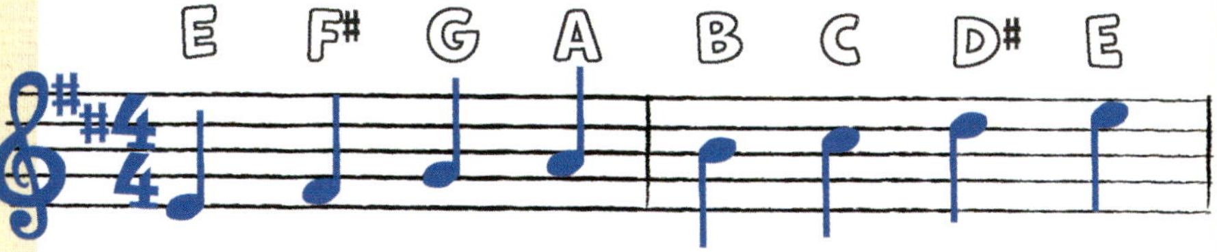

Pssst!
Although scales can help with songwriting, you don't have to use them if you'd rather not.

10 How to write lyrics

Lyrics are the words to a song.
Sometimes they rhyme. Sometimes they tell a story. Sometimes they express how the writer really, truly feels.

Fancy writing your own lyrics? Just jot down your ideas and feelings in a notebook whenever you get a chance.

You might love your pet cat. You might hate tidying your room. You might feel passionate about protecting the planet ... Anything goes!

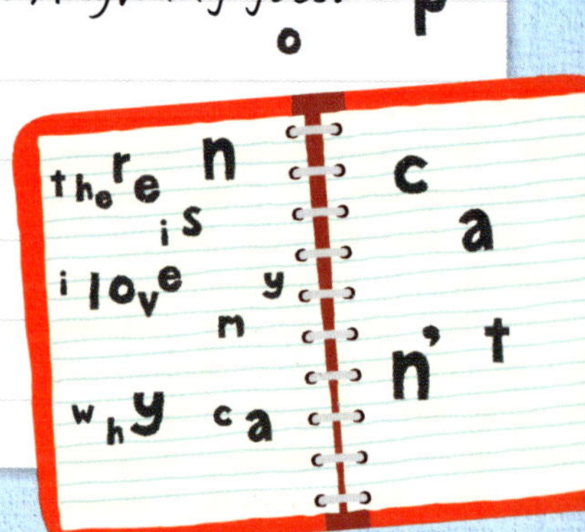

LALA

Verses and choruses

A chorus is usually the catchy bit repeated throughout the song. The verses usually contain the supporting ideas.

Rhyme time!

Some songs use full rhymes.
For example: "say" and "way"

Many songs use half-rhymes.
For example: "star" and "heart"

Other songs use repetition.
For example: "I can't stop, I can't stop …"

There are no rules with lyric writing. You can do whatever you like!

t i e

"I love coming up with a theme or title then turning it into a song. It's even more enjoyable to write music with your friends!"

Oh My Empress, singer-songwriter

Imagine you're a music star

WHO'S IN YOUR BAND?

ARE YOU A SOLO ARTIST?

WHAT'S YOUR ARTIST/BAND NAME?

WHAT TYPE OF MUSIC DO YOU PLAY?

Do you write your own songs?

WHERE DO YOU REHEARSE?

DO YOU SING OR PLAY AN INSTRUMENT?

WHAT'S ON YOUR RIDER?

WHAT'S THE TITLE OF YOUR FIRST SINGLE?

"I started my first band with my school friends. We taught ourselves our instruments and sounded hideous at first. But after loads of rehearsals, we sounded like a proper band!"

James Swabey, guitarist, Burn The Fleet

11 Making a music video

SEAT
11

Pick a theme

Most music videos have a main theme. This could be anything from making a new friend to remembering a favourite holiday.

Choose a look

- **Live-action shots** – where artists engage in scenes that tell a story.
- **Live-action dance** – featuring dancers performing a cool, choreographed routine.
- **Animation** – ranging from hand-drawn illustrations to the latest special effects.

"We were filmed walking through the streets of Brighton. We wore cool clothes and acted like the camera wasn't there. It went so well with the music!"

Luke Stone, guitarist, Stone Groove Collective

Which look would you choose?

SEAT

12 I'm with the brand!

SEAT 12

Ever been to a concert? Then you've probably walked past a merchandise stall. You might have even bought yourself a poster or T-shirt.

Selling merchandise is super-important to artists. In fact, it can even be their main way of making money!

LIAN
ZOE BARKER
SPLAT SPIN WHIRL
KILLIAN
SPLAT SPIN WHIRL
WORLD TOUR
DUENDE DUENDE
KILLIAN
FINLAY WILLIAMS
DUENDE DUENDE
LIVE TOUR
FINLAY WILLIAMS
THE HEART MURMURS
FINLAY WILLIAMS
DUENDE

Going on tour

Check out these awesome music venues! Maybe you'll tour them yourself one day?

Madison Square Garden
New York, USA

Allianz Parque
São Paulo, Brazil

New Afrika Shrine
Lagos, Nigeria

The O2
London, UK

Mercedes-Benz Arena
Shanghai, China

Sydney Opera House
Sydney, Australia

13 You already are a music maker!

SEAT 13

Sometimes the best things in life are the simple things: hearing an amazing tune, writing down a new idea, **belting** out your favourite song ...

You don't have to know loads about music to get involved – the most important thing is how it makes you feel.

Read about it, listen to it, learn to play it, fake it 'til you make it … Whatever you do with music, just enjoy it!

This book is full of examples to inspire you. You might even want to recommend it to a friend.

There's a beat inside every one of us – so what are you waiting for? You already *are* a music maker!

Five ways to get involved

Keep a journal about your favourite songs.

Ask your parent or school about learning an instrument.

Write your own lyrics – or a whole tune!

Design your own artist/band logo.

Start a band with your friends!

Glossary

amp (amplifier) a device that boosts the volume of an electric instrument

belting singing with a loud and strong voice

fleeting doesn't last for a long time

frets metal bars along the guitar neck showing where to put your fingers on the strings

heartfelt emotional

K-pop pop music of South Korea

remix music that's electronically altered

Index

What will YOU be in the music industry?

START HERE

Wanna be on stage?

Yeah!

Wanna sing your heart out?

Totally!

Not really

Nah!

Fancy getting creative with words?

Yes way!

No way!

You're a SINGER!
You're a MUSICIAN!
You're a SONGWRITER!
Yep!
Wanna put your words to music?
Nope
You're a MUSIC JOURNALIST!
Yaaas!
You're a MANAGER!
Fancy managing the business side?
Nooo
You're a BOOKING AGENT!

Ideas for reading

Written by Gill Matthews
Primary Literacy Consultant

Reading objectives:

- check that the text makes sense to them, discuss their understanding and explain the meaning of words in context
- identify main ideas drawn from more than one paragraph and summarise these
- retrieve and record information from non-fiction

Spoken language objectives:

- use relevant strategies to build their vocabulary
- articulate and justify answers, arguments and opinions
- participate in discussions, presentations, performances, role play, improvisations and debates

Curriculum links: Model music: singing, composing

Interest words: simple, belting, inspire, design

Resources: musical instruments, recording equipment

Build a context for reading

- Ask children to look closely at the front cover of the book and to read the title. Ask what they think a music maker is. Encourage them to support their responses with reasons.
- Read the back-cover blurb. Discuss what information they think they will find in the book.
- Point out that this is an information book. Ask children what features they would expect to find in the book.
- Ask them to turn to the contents page. Discuss the purpose and organisation of a contents.
- Ask children to use the contents to find the chapter called *Anyone can make music ...*